The First Day of Forever

By Kristi L. Necochea
& Nancy L. Dryburgh

Illustrations by Justine Dantzer

THE FRIENDS FOREVER GIRLS™ COLLECTION

The Friends Forever Girls™ Collection
Published by Inspire U., LLC
Copyright © 2007 by Inspire U., LLC

Questions or comments? Visit our Website at
Friendsforevergirls.com

ISBN-13: 978-09792361-0-5 hardcover
ISBN-13: 978-09792361-3-6 softcover

Library of Congress Control Number: 2008925568

Manufactured in the United States of America
2 3 4 5 6 7 – BP – 13 12 11 10 09 08

*To my husband for believing; our three beautiful
children for inspiring; and to my sisters, who will
always be my friends forever girls ~ K.L.N.*

*To John, the light of my life, and to
our wonderful daughters, Kate and Mandi.
All my love ~ N.L.D.*

Thank you for choosing to read The First
Day of Forever. It has been my dream to
create *The Friends Forever Girls*™ collection
of dolls and books, and I hope you like
them as much as I do!

Kristi L. Necochea

Chapter One

Marlee was deep asleep in her comfy canopy bed with pink cotton sheets when her nose began to tickle. Still lost in a dream, she lazily brought her right arm up and brushed the back of her hand across her nose. The tickle stopped and Marlee turned with a sigh and burrowed back down into her quilted comforter. A moment passed and the tickle returned even stronger.

She sat straight up in bed and giggled. She

opened her eyes just in time to see a brightly colored butterfly swoop out the bedroom window. "And good morning to you!" Marlee called. "You're better than an alarm clock." Ten-year-old Marlee was not a quick waker-upper, so Bella often helped her get up by tickling her nose.

Marlee knew her friendship with Bella was special- even more so because she lived on a street named Butterfly Lane. "Oh, Bella," Marlee giggled again as the butterfly swooped back and fluttered outside her window, "just give me a minute."

Marlee stretched her arms high over her head and twisted back and forth, letting out a good long yawn. She sniffed, then sniffed again. The cool air smelled so good.... She closed her blue eyes tight, tossed back her head, and breathed deeply. "Yep!" she announced, "fall is definitely here!"

Marlee loved autumn. Ever since she could remember, it had been her favorite season. She loved it for lots of reasons. "There's baking apple pie with Mom," she said to herself, "and raking leaves into big piles with Dad and the boys so we can jump on top of them." She smiled and continued, "There's carving pumpkins and trick or treating…

"Oh!" she exclaimed, stopping herself. Jumping out of bed, Marlee ran to the window and pushed aside the yellow, pink, and lavender curtains. She knelt on the cushion of her window seat, leaned as far as she could out the window, and peered down Butterfly Lane. This was a big day in the neighborhood. It was Saturday and she was expecting to see a moving truck.

Marlee's best friend, Natalie, lived across the street. Natalie's mom had told the girls that the family who bought the house two doors down from Natalie was moving in today. Marlee knew that Natalie was hoping a girl their age would be part of that family. Marlee had told Natalie that she hoped so too, but secretly she was a little nervous.

Marlee could hear her brothers downstairs eating breakfast and noisily making plans for the day. Their voices mixed with the sound of her mom and dad as they playfully sang along with the radio. Looking again out her bedroom window, Marlee decided she was not ready to go down to breakfast just yet. She wanted to see that moving truck the very moment it arrived!

"Hey, Natalie!" Marlee yelled and waved as she saw her friend walk outside in her pj's to grab the newspaper. Natalie read the comics every morning. "Natalie!" Marlee yelled again. Natalie was carrying a big glass of orange juice. When she heard her name, she spun around so fast that half the juice sloshed out of her glass and spilled onto her white fuzzy slippers.

Marlee laughed so loud that Natalie finally noticed her leaning out her bedroom window. "Yuck!" Natalie groaned as she shook the juice off her hand. She waved quickly, grabbed the newspaper, and ran back into her house.

Marlee giggled. She loved being best friends with Natalie because they had so much in common. They were practically inseparable. In fact, the neighbors had taken to calling them Salt 'n Pepper because if they saw one girl they knew the other couldn't be far behind.

Although they had a lot in common, in some ways they were different. Natalie did well in all kinds of sports, but her favorites were swimming and diving. She loved the water and told Marlee that someday she wanted to swim with dolphins. Marlee wished that she could swim or run or catch as well as her best friend. Sometimes Marlee felt discouraged about her lack of athletic ability. Then her dad would remind her, "Try your best. Be the best Marlee you can be." This made her feel better. She also knew that Natalie admired her talents, too. In fact, Natalie often asked Marlee to draw special pictures for her to decorate her room.

That's what makes being best friends with Natalie great, thought Marlee. We have a lot in common, but we're also very different. I like it that way. She wondered what would happen to their friendship if a new girl moved into the neighborhood. Oh well, she thought, I'm sure everything will be okay.

Chapter Two

Marlee's little brother, Jake, shouted up the stairs, "Marlee, the truck is here!" Marlee, who'd been lost in thought, eagerly looked out the window. Sure enough, she thought, there it is. And there's Natalie jumping up and down, pointing at the truck. Gee, she's dressed and I'm still in my pajamas!

Marlee scrambled. She splashed water on her face and put on her shirt, skirt, and boots. She grabbed her jacket, raced down the stairs, and pushed past her big brother, Pete, who was blocking the front door. "You're a better door than a window!" she shouted as she ran down the sidewalk. The burly truck driver had unloaded nine boxes and a computer table by the time Marlee got to Natalie's house.

Natalie threw her arm across Marlee's shoulders and whispered, "Do you think...maybe?" With that, the driver rolled a glittery pink bike down the moving truck's ramp. Natalie hugged Marlee. "A new friend! A new girl in our neighborhood!" she cheered. "I can hardly wait to meet her and find out where she's from and what she's like and what she likes to do and if she has any brothers or sisters and this is going to be so great!"

Just as Natalie stopped to take a breath, a dark blue car pulled up in front of the moving van. When the car door opened, out jumped a scruffy white dog that ran as fast as his little legs could carry him straight to Marlee and Natalie. As he circled them, barking in sharp yips, they heard a girl's voice call loudly, "Scout, Scout!" A girl with long black hair hopped out of the car and rushed toward them.

The dog turned, ran, and leaped into her arms, burrowing its head into her soft sweater. "Hi, I'm Reina," she said with a bright smile as she walked up to the girls.

Right away, Marlee noticed that Reina was about the same age as them. "Hi," she and Natalie said in unison. "I'm Marlee and I live in that house on the corner," she said, pointing to the top of the lane.

"And I'm Natalie and I live two houses up from you," Natalie said. "I've lived here since I was three. This is a great neighborhood. I like

your dog. We can't have a dog because my dad's allergic to them. We've got a fish. Your dog's cute!"

She leaned over to pat him in Reina's arms. "Do you have any brothers or sisters? I have an older brother and sister. They call me motor mouth, and..."

Finally, Natalie noticed Reina's face and stopped. Reina was looking at her with amazement. Turning to Marlee, she giggled. All three girls burst out laughing at the same time. Scout yipped as if he were laughing, too.

Marlee, wiping tears from her eyes, stopped laughing long enough to say to Reina, "Don't pay any attention. Sometimes she gets going and can't stop!"

Then, in a colorful swirl of autumn leaves, a butterfly darted overhead. Reina watched as the butterfly flew closer and closer in circles around the girls. Marlee smiled and said to Reina, "Oh, and you can call her Bella!"

"Bella means 'beautiful' in Italian," said Natalie.

Reina asked, "Is she…is she…your pet?"

Natalie and Marlee exchanged a look. "No, she's not really our pet. She's our special friend," said Marlee.

"Now she'll be your special friend, too," Natalie chimed in.

At that moment, with Bella flying gracefully overhead, Marlee began to feel that this was the beginning of a fun new friendship. I must have been worried about nothing, she thought as she looked at Natalie and Reina.

Chapter Three

A whole week had gone by since Marlee met her new neighbor. Marlee was putting the breakfast dishes away when she heard Scout barking in the backyard. "Scout's here again," she shouted to her mom as she picked up the phone to call Reina. "Hi, Reina. It's me, Marlee. Scout's in our yard."

"Not again!" moaned Reina. "The phone's been ringing off the hook all week. Even with a fence, Scout keeps finding new ways to get out of our backyard."

"It's good that you put your phone number on his collar. It's been a quick way for you to meet almost everyone on Butterfly Lane," chuckled Marlee. "I'll bring him right over."

Marlee lifted Scout into her arms and walked across the street. As she passed Natalie's house, she felt uneasy. It's great having a new friend, she thought, but I'm still afraid that Natalie might like Reina better than me. What if I get left out? What if they go to the mall and don't invite me? As she approached Reina's house, Marlee tried to push those thoughts out of her mind.

"Hi, Marlee. Thanks so much for bringing Scout back," Reina said. Marlee looked beyond the front door, admiring a beautiful quilt on the living room wall. Reina seemed to read her mind. "Oh, my nana made that. She loves to quilt. Would you like to see the rest of our house? We finished painting and finally got everything out of the boxes."

"Sure," answered Marlee. Scout led the tour. The last place they visited was Reina's room. As they opened the door, the first thing Marlee saw was dozens of stuffed animals scattered on the bed. She then noticed several bookshelves. "My gosh, Reina. You must have over a hundred books!"

"They're mostly about animals," Reina explained. "I just love animals. Someday I want to be a veterinarian so I can work with them all the time."

Marlee suddenly had an idea. "Thanks for showing me your house, Reina," she said. "I have to go home and do some chores, but I want to show you a special place this afternoon. How about if I get Natalie and pick you up after lunch?"

"That sounds great," Reina replied. "My dad just started a fire, so I'm going take a nap by the fireplace with Scout. See you later."

Chapter Four

"**Reina! Reina!**" called Marlee and Natalie from Reina's front steps.

"Huh?" Reina answered in a sleepy voice. "Who's there?"

"It's Marlee and me," called Natalie, trying to look through the window in the front door. As Reina opened the door, Natalie continued, "Are you ready? Is it okay for you to go? Want to take your bike? Your bike's beautiful and new…mine's really old. It's a hand-me-down from my sister, and anyway the tire's flat. My dad's really busy and hasn't had time to fix it, so I haven't ridden a bike in a long time, although I really like to ride. I like pink a lot too, and your bike is pink… it's just great!" blurted Natalie.

Reina put Scout on the floor, rubbed her eyes with her fist, and asked, "What? Where are we going?"

"Nana's Grove!" said the two girls excitedly.

"We're going to show you the fabulous, spectacular, wonderful place at the farthest end of Butterfly Lane," Marlee continued. "It has everything! Just wait and see!"

"But best of all," said Natalie, "it has Picasso."

"Picasso?" asked Reina. "What's Picasso?"

"Well," replied Marlee, "besides the fact that it's the name of a famous painter, it's also the name of my horse!"

"You've got a horse and he's a famous painter?" Reina kidded.

"No, silly," Marlee answered, "his name is…" Then, realizing Reina's joke, she stopped herself. "Oh, I get it!" All the girls laughed.

"I can't wait to meet him," said Reina. "Can Scout come, too?" Scout yipped and jumped playfully at Reina's feet.

"I think it'll be fine," answered Marlee. "Picasso is so big, he won't mind such a little dog."

Reina pulled the heavy wooden door shut as they turned to go. "Don't you have to tell somebody you're leaving?" asked Natalie.

"Oh yeah, I almost forgot. My parents took my brother and sister to buy a basketball hoop for the backyard. I'll just run inside and leave a note."

When she came back out, Reina grabbed her bike and the girls set out. Reina rode slowly next to Natalie and Marlee as they walked with Scout scampering along next to them. "Where did you live before?" Natalie asked Reina.

"Albuquerque, New Mexico," answered Reina. "I loved it there. My friends and I used to do everything together."

Reina hopped off her bike and began walking it. Every once in a while, she picked up an especially colorful leaf and tucked it in her backpack.

"Reina, you never go anywhere without that backpack," said Natalie. "You're just like Marlee."

"I like being prepared," Reina explained, "and you never know when you might need something."

Marlee understood this because she never went anywhere without her sketch pad and pencils. Marlee thought that her love of drawing was just like Reina's love of animals and Natalie's fondness for the water.

They had almost reached the gated entrance to Nana's Grove when out of a tumble of leaves Bella appeared. Like an animated leaf, Bella swooped down over their heads just as a kind voice said, "Hi girls. I see Bella's with you today. Who's your new friend?"

"This is Reina and her dog, Scout," said Natalie. "Reina, this is Nana Rosa. She has the greenest thumb of anyone I know. See all the different flowers in her garden? Aren't they pretty? Over there in the greenhouse is where she grows the most beautiful orchids. She works at the nursery in town and..." Natalie stopped herself. Reina, Marlee, and Nana Rosa laughed.

Nana Rosa stepped over to Scout and bent down. "Well, Reina, this must be your owner. Scout, how nice to meet you." She stood up and smiled at Reina. As Reina giggled, Natalie and Marlee looked at each other, rolled their eyes and smiled.

Reina said, "Maybe you're right. Sometimes I think he does own me!"

"So where are you from, Reina?" Nana Rosa asked.

"Albuquerque!" Natalie and Marlee replied at the same time.

"Jinx!" yelled Marlee.

Nana Rosa asked Reina how she liked living on Butterfly Lane. "Oh, I love it so far, but I miss my friends back home."

"When I was almost your age, my parents

moved our family from a little town in Italy to the United States."

"Were you scared?" asked Reina.

"Oh, it was a little frightening, but very exciting, too. I missed my old friends and school, but I was happy to meet new kids. You see, Reina, you never want to forget your old friends. They'll always be very special, and you'll want to keep in touch with them. In fact, my best friend is a girl I met way back in first grade. We'll always be close, even though we live thousands of miles apart. When I came to this country, I met a new group of girls, and we're still friends, too.

"When I was young we used to sing a great song about old and new friends. Do you want to hear it?"

All three girls nodded.

Nana Rosa continued, "It goes like this:
>*Make new friends, but keep the old*
>*One is silver and the other's gold*
>*A circle is round and has no end*
>*That's how long I'll be your friend*
>*Across the land, across the sea*
>*Friends forever we'll always be!"*

Nana Rosa added, "I'm sure I'll be friends with them forever."

"I think we'll be friends forever, too," Natalie said to Marlee and Reina.

But what will happen to Salt 'n Pepper? Marlee thought. How will this change my friendship with Natalie?

Natalie skipped over to Reina and Marlee and took their hands. "Well, that's a circle of gold if I ever saw one," Nana Rosa exclaimed.

As the girls stood holding hands in a tight circle, Marlee looked up and saw Bella fly over their heads. She smiled.

"Hey, Bella," Natalie called out. "Guess what? We're the FRIENDS FOREVER GIRLS!"

Chapter Five

"**Well, I've got to** get going," said Nana Rosa, glancing at her watch. "I have to get to the store, and I know you're all getting antsy to have Reina meet Picasso, right?"

"Right!" the girls yelled.

"Oh, I almost forgot. I'd better get his rose!" Nana Rosa produced a small pair of garden shears from her pocket. Choosing a soft red rose from a nearby bush, she clipped the stem and handed it to Marlee. "Goodbye, girls. Welcome to the neighborhood, Reina."

Scout barked. "Oh, and goodbye to you, too, Scout." Nana Rosa patted the dog's curly white head. "Don't you be too rough on Picasso! He's quite sensitive for a big boy!" With that, she crossed the yard to her driveway and drove off in a flurry of leaves that fanned out behind her red pickup truck.

As the girls walked through the gate and down the path into Nana's Grove, they passed a big patch of grass. "That's a perfect spot for playing baseball," Reina exclaimed.

"Do you play?" said Natalie. "My dad coaches! Maybe you could be on my team."

As Natalie and Reina talked excitedly about their favorite sports and what positions they liked to play, Marlee walked behind them in silence, feeling like the odd one out. Reina steered her bike down the path and interrupted Marlee's thoughts. "I like her. I like her a lot!"

"Who?" asked Marlee quietly.

"Nana Rosa," replied Natalie as she looked over her shoulder and waited for Marlee to catch up.

"But why did she give you a rose for your horse?" asked Reina.

Marlee said, "Well, one day Picasso got loose and found his way to the entrance of Nana's Grove. He managed to poke his nose through the front gate and before anybody noticed he had eaten a whole bush of Nana Rosa's award-winning roses!"

"She doesn't have the name Rosa for nothing," quipped Natalie.

"That's for sure," said Marlee. "Nana Rosa

decided right then and there that if Picasso liked roses that much, she was going to grow him his very own rosebush! So she did. They're even called 'Picasso Roses'."

"She grows roses for your horse 'cause he likes to eat them- and the roses have the same name as your horse?" Reina asked in amazement.

"Yep," nodded Marlee, "pretty special, huh?"

The girls crossed the meadow and walked into the stable yard. "How many horses live here?" asked Reina.

"Five," said Marlee as she led the girls past a stack of hay bales to a row of wooden stalls. "Four of them belong to Mr. Taylor, and he lets us keep Picasso here."

Suddenly a large golden head with a long blond mane peered at them through the top of a blue stall door. "Picasso!" Marlee called. He shook his head and whinnied in response.

"Let's go!" cried Natalie. Reina dropped her bike on its side and they all ran to Picasso's stall.

Marlee held the rose carefully as Natalie unlocked the latch and opened the door. Out strode a gorgeous palomino with white socks and a mane so light it looked almost white. "Wow," sighed Reina appreciatively.

"Look, even his eyelashes are blond,"

Natalie said.

Picasso seemed to enjoy all the attention. He put his left leg out straight, curled his right leg under his chest, and bowed his head in a "curtsy." "You're a big, beautiful boy," Marlee said as she held out the rose. Picasso sniffed it delicately as if to make sure it was from his rosebush, then woofed it down in two bites.

"Picasso is amazing," gushed Reina. "You're so lucky to have him, Marlee."

"I sure am. He's the best horse ever."

While Reina and Natalie patted his smooth coat and velvet nose, Marlee got busy collecting the gear. "Have you ever ridden before?" she asked.

Reina, wide-eyed, shook her head. "No, but I would love to learn."

"Then today might be your lucky day! I might even let you do the 'mucking out' afterwards," said Marlee with a wink to Natalie, who hid a quick smile behind her hand.

"Mucking out. What's that?" asked Reina.

"Oh, you'll love it," Natalie answered with a chuckle. "It's lots of fun. I usually do it, but seeing as how you're new and all...maybe just for today I'll let you do it."

Reina made a face like she wasn't quite sure she'd like the job.

"I guess you don't know much about horses," said Marlee.

"I've read a little," Reina replied.

"First," said Marlee in a serious tone, enjoying her role as instructor, "we take him over to the cross ties to be brushed and saddled." Marlee led Picasso down the hallway and clipped both sides of his halter to the lead ropes that hung from the walls.

The girls followed Marlee. They in turn were followed by a cautious Scout, who stopped at the stable entrance, sat down in the dirt, and stared at Picasso. Reina walked back to the entrance and crouched next to Scout. "I know you've never seen a horse before," she said, petting his head softly. "It's okay, don't be scared." She stood up and walked back to Picasso.

Marlee handed a small oval brush with a strap on the back to Reina and a similar one to Natalie. "Now, this is how it's done," she said briskly as she started to brush. Next Marlee took a striped blanket from a peg on the wall, folded it neatly in half, and carefully tossed it over Picasso's back. "Natalie, can you bring me the saddle?" she asked as she pulled a sturdy wooden mounting block to Picasso's left side.

"Oof!" Natalie lifted the heavy, brown saddle

and brought it to Marlee.

"Wow," said Reina. "I've only seen saddles like this on TV or in the movies. It's beautiful." She ran her hand over the edge, which was carved with garlands of daisies and tiny hearts. Then she rubbed her fingers along the saddle's neck, where the leather looked like twisted rope.

Marlee climbed on the block next to Picasso and in one motion placed the saddle on his back.

"Watch this, Reina," Natalie said. She reached under Picasso's belly, making sure the saddle was centered. Then she grabbed and tightened the girth around Picasso's middle.

"Natalie, I can show Reina the rest," Marlee said. Taking care of horses was one thing Marlee could do better than any of her friends, and she wanted to show Reina her skills. "Over there on the peg is the bridle. Can you bring it to me, please?" she asked Reina. Reina found it and handed it to Marlee. Picasso took the bit as Marlee bridled him. "Now we have to make sure that the bit isn't too high in his mouth," she explained as she checked its placement.

"Wow, Marlee, you sure know a lot about horses," Reina said.

"Thanks, Reina," responded Marlee, feeling good about the compliment. "Would you like to take Picasso's reins and walk him outside in a circle a couple of times?"

"Would I!" cried Reina. Picasso whinnied as Reina guided him around the stable yard.

"Now we need to re-cinch him," Marlee announced, "and then we can go. I'd better ride him first to make sure he's okay with everything, and then maybe you both can try a ride." Marlee climbed onto a mounting block in the yard. Placing her left foot firmly in the stirrup, she swung gracefully into the saddle.

After she mounted, Marlee leaned down and patted Picasso's neck, praising him softly. Picasso huffed a contented response.

The girls left the stable yard together and followed the dirt path into the flowered meadow. Reina went first on her glistening bike, followed by Marlee on her golden horse and Natalie sauntering along, carrying Scout.

Chapter Six

It was mid afternoon, the sun was still shining and Picasso seemed delighted to be out of his stall. They hadn't gone far before Marlee said, "Okay. Natalie, I think he's ready for you."

"No, Marlee," Natalie replied. "I've ridden Picasso tons of times and I think Reina should go first."

Marlee stopped, a little surprised at Natalie's generosity. "Oh, okay," Marlee stammered, once again wondering if Natalie was starting to like Reina more than her. "Sure, I - I guess Reina can go first." She swung her right leg carefully over Picasso's rump, released her left foot from the stirrup, and dropped to the ground. "Okay, now stand still, Picasso, and we'll boost you up, Reina." Marlee gave her some more tips on mounting, and up and over Reina went onto Picasso's golden back.

"This is like a wish come true," said Reina. She looked excited, but also a little scared. "It's really high up here," she said.

Reina took the reins, settled in as instructed, and held on tight. "When did you get Picasso?" she asked.

"Some friends of my parents own a farm, and we visited them about three years ago," Marlee said. "They had some horses for sale and one of them was Picasso. When we stood on the fence railing to watch them, Picasso was the first one to come over to my brothers and me. He was so friendly that Dad decided to make Picasso our family's horse."

The girls continued to talk about horses as they neared the edge of the woods on the far side of Nana's Grove.

"Guess we have to turn around and go back," sighed Natalie.

"Why?" asked Marlee, a bit more loudly than needed.

"Because we're not allowed to go into the woods unless we tell our parents first," responded Natalie, turning to Marlee. "And besides, it's getting late and we have to get home."

"Oh, don't be so grumpy." Marlee frowned. She was enjoying being in charge and didn't want to give it up so quickly.

"Let's go to the pond. I want to draw a picture of the two of you on Picasso's back. It won't take long-it's not too far. Come on, it'll be fun. I really want to do this," she finished, out of breath. Marlee realized she didn't sound a bit like herself. Instead she sounded strange and definitely bossy. But at that moment she didn't care.

Both Reina and Natalie looked at Marlee in surprise. "What will our parents say?" asked Natalie.

Marlee realized she had forgotten to ask her parents if she could go to Nana's Grove. She knew they would be upset, but she shrugged off those thoughts. "Well, they won't have to know," she stated defiantly. "Come on, let's hurry! I think there's a shortcut this way."

With that, Marlee rode the bike into the woods. Reina and Natalie reluctantly followed. Sharp, thorny bushes poked their legs, and branches and twigs snarled Picasso's mane. Marlee called for them to keep up with her as she continued into the woods. She didn't notice that Reina looked uneasy on top of Picasso or that Natalie's face reflected her worry. Even Scout, in Natalie's arms, started to growl.

By the time they reached the pond, everyone but Marlee was acting upset and nervous. Marlee ignored the questioning looks and the quiet that had settled upon them. She was intent on drawing her picture. "Here," she pointed, "is the perfect spot, right here under this old oak tree. Natalie, you climb up behind Reina and then walk Picasso out into the water. This will be my

34

best drawing ever!"

"Marlee, we really shouldn't be here," muttered Natalie as she put Scout on the ground and climbed onto Picasso behind Reina.

Ignoring Natalie's comment, Marlee continued, "Okay, Picasso, now just go out into the water, and Reina, you pull on the reins when

I tell you to stop. Got it?"

"I don't know, Marlee, I'm not sure about this." Reina said.

"Oh, come on," Marlee coaxed, "you'll be fine." Taking her pad of paper and pencils out of her backpack, Marlee continued, "He's a trained trail horse and he's used to going into the water. Go on! Go on!" Marlee commanded Picasso, giving him a slap on his behind. Picasso, startled, walked swiftly down the muddy bank into the chilly water.

At that exact moment, a red squirrel jumped from a pile of dead leaves. With a loud bark, Scout raced off to chase the squirrel. Picasso reared up at the sudden sound and plunged further into the pond as Reina and Natalie held on as tightly as they could. A dark tree limb stuck out into the water, looking like a snake ready to strike. Spooked, Picasso frantically spun around in circles, churning up silt that turned the water a muddy brown. Natalie flew off the horse and disappeared into the water!

Marlee, who had been frozen in shock, dropped her pad and pencils and ran to the edge of the water. Reina held onto the reins as she and Marlee screamed for Natalie.

"Reina, hold on!" Marlee yelled. With tears

in her eyes, she thought, Where's Natalie? Both girls searched the muddy water, which had risen to Picasso's belly. Although he had stopped struggling, he was sweating, his eyes were wide, and he was snorting as he breathed.

"Natalie, Natalie!" screamed Marlee again. Her thoughts were screaming, too. Natalie could be drowned…The water's rising…Picasso's probably hurt…Reina's scared to death and Scout is lost! How had everything gone so wrong so fast? How was she going to get them out of this mess?

"We need help and we need it now!" Reina yelled.

Chapter Seven

Whoosh! Natalie's blond head, now filthy from the dirty water, rose from behind Picasso. As she gulped for air, she yelled, "He's okay! He's not hurt. He's just stuck in the mud. He's okay, but he's going to need help to get out," she repeated.

"Natalie!" Marlee and Reina screamed. "You're alive!"

"You're alive...you're alive," stammered Marlee gratefully.

"Sure," Natalie grinned. "After I got thrown off, I dove down there to make sure he wasn't hurt."

When Natalie climbed out of the water, Marlee threw her arms around her, mud and all. "I thought, I mean, we thought," she said, correcting herself with a glance at Reina's sad face, "we'd lost you." Her voice trembled.

"No way!" replied Natalie. "You know I'm a really good swimmer. The water's a little cold, though."

Marlee pulled herself together. "Um, Picasso is stuck, you said? Well, we can handle that, right?"

Marlee thought a second. "Reina, you're doing a great job with Picasso. Can you just stay with him until we get help?"

"Sure," Reina said as she stroked Picasso's neck, "but somebody's got to find Scout."

Marlee picked up Reina's bike and started to get on. "I'll ride back and get help, and Natalie, you stay here and look for Scout, okay?"

Marlee took one look at Natalie's face and stopped cold. Natalie reached out and put her muddy hands on the white rubber handlebars and said evenly, "Let me go."

"But you're all wet and it's getting colder!" protested Marlee.

"I'm a faster rider and we need help right away," Natalie said firmly. With a determined look, she jumped on Reina's bike and took off.

"Go to my house first!" shouted Marlee. "Someone should be home."

Natalie, pedaling as fast as she could up the slippery, leafy slope, yelled back over her shoulder, "I'll be back as soon as I can!" and was quickly out of sight.

"Marlee, please, please, look for Scout," begged Reina. Marlee looked hard at both Reina and Picasso. The water had risen to Reina's calves. Why is the water rising? Marlee wondered. Then she realized with a jolt of fear that Picasso was sinking! Her horse was sinking in the mud, and the more time that passed, the harder it would be to free him.

She didn't want to leave Picasso, but Marlee knew she needed to find Scout. She felt like it was her fault that this whole thing had happened and her fault that Scout was lost. "Just keep doing what you're doing," she reassured Reina. "I'll go find Scout."

"Before you go, Marlee, there's an apple in my backpack. Throw it to me for Picasso."

Marlee found the big green apple but hesitated. "I'm not good at pitching," she admitted. This time Reina reassured Marlee. "Go ahead, Marlee. I know you can do it."

Marlee carefully gauged the distance and threw. She managed to toss the apple right to Reina, who caught it with ease. As Marlee took off to find Scout, she turned back toward Reina. "Reina, I'm so sorry I got us into this mess. I'm sorry about everything. I know I've been acting strange, but I've just been afraid that you would become better friends with Natalie and that I'd be left out."

Reina smiled. "Are you kidding? We're the Friends Forever Girls!"

Just then Bella appeared and landed lightly on Picasso's ear. "Look, Reina, Bella is here to keep you company."

Reina smiled at her and leaned over and offered Picasso the apple. Marlee returned the smile and took off running in the direction they'd seen Scout chase the squirrel.

"Scout...here boy...Scout, come here boy!"

Chapter Eight

Several things happened all at once. First, Marlee appeared from behind a patch of trees holding a wiggly white ball of fluff. "I found him, Reina, I found Scout!"

Reina smiled with relief. "Thank you, Marlee. I'm so glad he's safe."

"Look, I found a rope hanging on the fence post," Marlee continued. "I think we can use it to help free Picasso."

"Great idea, Marlee. Toss me one end and I'll tie it around Picasso's neck."

Marlee made a lasso at one end of the rope and threw it to Reina. Just as Reina got the rope around Picasso's neck, Natalie rode up on the bike. She was grinning and still caked in mud. Over Natalie's head they saw three men walking toward them. "We're coming! We're coming!" Reina's father called out.

"We'll be right there," added Marlee's dad. "Is everyone okay?"

"We're alright, Dad, but Picasso's stuck," Marlee shouted to her father, who was wearing tall fisherman boots. "I found this rope and we put it around his neck to help pull him out."

"That was smart thinking, girls," Marlee's dad said. When everyone reached the pond, Marlee's dad waded into the water toward Reina and Picasso while the others waited on the embankment. "Do you want to be lifted off before we pull him out?" asked Marlee's dad, "or do you want to finish your ride?"

"Would it be alright if I rode him out?" Reina asked.

"What do you think, Picasso, old boy? Can Reina ride you out?"

Picasso tossed his head up and down in what passed for a pretty good "yes."

Reina rode him as the three men tried to pull and coax Picasso out of the mud. When this proved unsuccessful, Reina's dad got in the water, too, leaning his back against Picasso's right flank to help lift him free. Marlee and Natalie took his place at the edge of the pond and pulled on the rope, along with Natalie's dad. Scout kept very still and watched while Marlee encouraged her horse, "Come on, Picasso, you can do it!"

Picasso worked hard to free his legs, and with a big sucking sound, he finally broke out of the thick mud and walked unsteadily up the slippery bank. Marlee gave the horse a big hug.

The girls and their fathers headed out of the

forest and back to the stable.

"Well, that's definitely enough for today," Marlee's dad said to her.

"Dad," Marlee spoke softly as she reached for his hand, "I'm sorry for not letting you know where I was."

"You know, Marlee, the family rule is you need to tell your mom or me where you're going. We had no idea where you were. We've been looking all over for you."

"I know Dad, I made a big mistake."

"I hope you learned your lesson today and don't let it happen again."

"I promise, Dad, it won't," replied Marlee. She couldn't believe what a strange day it had been.

Back at the stables, Marlee and her father carefully groomed Picasso, got him settled with a bag of oats, and wrapped him in a blanket. "You'll be just fine, won't you, boy?" said Marlee.

While Marlee and her dad took care of Picasso, Reina's dad used saddle soap to clean the saddle gear, showing Reina how to do it. "I used to help my uncle take care of his horses when I was your age, Reina. This sure is a beautiful saddle." When he finished, Reina showed him the correct pegs and places to hang the gear.

Natalie and her father shoveled out and

cleaned the horses' stalls, and Reina finally got to
see what "mucking out" meant. Reina offered to
help with the dirty job, but Natalie just smiled and
said, "Oh, it's okay. I'm dressed for it. And anyway,
it's kind of fun to do it with my dad."

It was late and quite cool by the time they all
gave Picasso his final "goodnight" pats and closed
his stall door tight. Stopping for a moment,
Marlee's dad pulled up the collar on his jacket.
"Autumn is definitely here," he said.

When they got to the gate, Nana Rosa's cottage glowed with light. She met them with mugs of hot chocolate and invited them back to her home. "I heard you had a big adventure, girls, and I figured some hot cocoa would taste really good before you all went home."

The cocoa was yummy and quickly warmed them up. Reina said, "Marlee, that was really strange when Bella came to stay with Picasso and me. I wonder how she found us?"

"That's our Bella," answered Marlee. "She's always there when we need her. That's what makes her so special."

Marlee suddenly had an idea and quickly reached for her sketch pad and pencils. "You know," she said as she settled back into the sofa and motioned for her friends to join her, "I learned so much today and I'm so sorry for getting us into such a big mess. I realize that even though I wanted to be a good friend, I wasn't being a good friend at all." She arranged the sketch pad on her lap. "I was thinking," she paused, "since we're going to be the Friends Forever Girls, how about if we make a promise to ourselves and to our friendship."

"That's a great idea," said Natalie.

"Here, look at this." Marlee took the pencil and

wrote the word BUTTERFLY in a vertical line on the piece of paper. She then began writing. Reina took the pencil and quickly added another line. In no time the girls added the promises that they wanted to use to guide their special friendship, their Friends Forever Girls friendship.

I promise to:

Be the best I can be
Use kindness and be fair
Tell the truth
Treat others the way I want to be treated
Encourage my friends
Respect myself and others
Find the courage to do what's right
Listen to others
    and remember...
You can do it!

As they all left Nana Rosa's house, the fathers walked ahead and the girls giggled among themselves, full of excitement for what was to come.

"I'm sure we'll remember today forever," smiled Marlee.

"And we'll have even greater adventures." said Natalie.

"And make lots more new friends," added Reina.

As the three girls and their fathers walked home, Bella landed on Marlee's shoulder. Marlee reached up and gently cupped her in her hand. "This turned out to be a great day," said Marlee. "Our friendship and our butterfly promises have made this the first day of forever!"

Here are some questions to discuss with your friends and parents, or to just think about on your own.

1. Why do you think Marlee had an uneasy feeling about Reina moving in? Do you think Natalie noticed?

2. Marlee expressed her fear of being left out by acting bossy. Can you think of other ways she could have expressed those feelings?

3. Marlee is good at drawing and writing, Natalie is good at sports and being a team player, and Reina is good at reading and caring for animals. What are you good at? What are some things your friends are good at?

4. How do you feel and act if you're not good at something?

5. Which of the Butterfly Promises do you think are most important? Which promises are the easiest for you to do? Which are the hardest?

6. Talk with your friends about the Butterfly Promises. What promises would help make your friendships extra-special?

7. Some families create a list of promises or rules that help everyone get along better. Talk with your parents to find out what they think of this idea. What promises would you want to include?